18796

B
SZO

Kustanowitz, Shulamit
E.

Henrietta Szold

$10.95

| DATE | | | |
|---|---|---|---|
| | | | |
| | | | |
| | | | |
| | | | |
| | | | |
| | | | |
| | | | |
| | | | |
| | | | |
| | | | |
| | | | |

WITHDRAWN

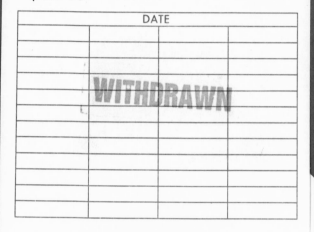

# HENRIETTA SZOLD
## ISRAEL'S HELPING HAND

*The Women of Our Time*® series

# HENRIETTA SZOLD

## ISRAEL'S HELPING HAND

BY SHULAMIT E. KUSTANOWITZ
Illustrated by Robert Masheris

VIKING

*Dedicated to my father,*
*Rabbi Benjamin H. Englander, z"l*
S.E.K.


*Special thanks to Judith Herschlag Muffs,*
*Director of Special Projects, Anti-Defamation League*

Viking
Published by the Penguin Group
Viking Penguin, a division of Penguin Books USA Inc.,
40 West 23rd Street, New York, New York 10010, U.S.A.
Penguin Books Ltd, 27 Wrights Lane, London W8 5TZ, England
Penguin Books Australia Ltd, Ringwood, Victoria, Australia
Penguin Books Canada Ltd, 2801 John Street, Markham, Ontario, Canada L3R 1B4
Penguin Books (N.Z.) Ltd, 182–190 Wairau Road, Auckland 10, New Zealand

Penguin Books Ltd, Registered Offices: Harmondsworth, Middlesex, England

First published in 1990 by Viking Penguin, a division of Penguin Books USA Inc.
1   3   5   7   9   10   8   6   4   2
Text copyright © Shulamit E. Kustanowitz, 1990
Illustrations copyright © Robert Masheris, 1990
All rights reserved

WOMEN OF OUR TIME® is a registered trademark of Viking Penguin,
a division of Penguin Books USA Inc.

LIBRARY OF CONGRESS CATALOGING IN PUBLICATION DATA
Kustanowitz, Shulamit E.    Henrietta Szold
by Shulamit Kustanowitz; illustrated by Robert Masheris.
p.   cm.—(Women of our time)
Summary: A biography of the leader who fought to improve the lives of Jewish people.
ISBN 0-670-82518-2
1. Szold, Henrietta, 1860–1945—Juvenile Literature.   2. Zionists—United States—
Biography—Juvenile literature.   [1. Szold, Henrietta, 1860–1945.   2. Zionists.
3. Jews—Biography.]   I. Masheris, Robert, ill.   II. Title.   III. Series.
DS151.S9K87 1990    320.5'4'095694092—dc20    [B] [92]   89-70656

Printed in the United States of America

# CONTENTS

# HENRIETTA SZOLD
## ISRAEL'S HELPING HAND

# 1

# In Her Father's Library

When she was young, Henrietta's favorite place in the whole world was her father's library. She loved to sit there, in her own little rocking chair, near her father's wide wood desk. As he sat there and studied, she would struggle to balance a huge book on her lap just like his. She would look up at him often, hoping he would explain his work to her.

She loved to do things with her father and he must have loved it, too, because he often took her with him. Early in the morning, they would visit people

who were sick. Later they would meet with members of their synagogue. Even when she was very young, Henrietta understood that he was the rabbi of the fastest-growing Jewish congregation in Baltimore, Maryland. He was an important man.

Her parents moved to Baltimore only a year before Henrietta was born. Benjamin Szold (say "zold") had been a rabbi in a town in Hungary, near Germany and Russia. Life in those countries was often difficult, and sometimes dangerous for Jews. Because Jews do not believe in Jesus as the messiah, some Christians did not like them or trust them. Some government laws did not allow Jews to own a business or to hold certain jobs. Some neighbors who were not Jewish attacked them or even killed them. This hating of Jews was called anti-Semitism.

Many government and church officials allowed this behavior. They blamed Jews for problems they could not possibly have caused or solved. They said it was the Jews' fault when there was too much rain, a cold winter, or the spread of sickness.

Rabbi Szold wanted to try life in America, the land where people were free to be different. In 1859, he married Sophie Schaar in Hungary. Soon they moved to a small house in Baltimore. Rabbi Szold became the rabbi of Congregation Oheb Shalom, which means "Lover of Peace."

Henrietta was born on December 21, 1860, the year Abraham Lincoln became president of the United States. She was named Chayaleh ("HI-ya-leh") after her grandmother—from the word *hai,* meaning "life" in Hebrew—but everyone always called her Henrietta. She was a pretty little girl, with a round face, big brown eyes, and dark hair.

She grew up learning to observe Jewish laws as her family did. As observant Jews, the Szolds ate only kosher food. To begin the Sabbath, their day of rest, Mrs. Szold lit candles every Friday at sundown. The family ate *hallah* ("HA-lah"), a braided bread, and served meals on their finest dishes and silverware.

When Henrietta and her mother went to services at the synagogue on Saturdays and holidays, they sat in the women's section. After services, the family had wonderful discussions at the dinner table. Then they would go visit friends, or take a long walk, or read, or nap. Their day of rest was over after the sun set Saturday evening.

Most of the people they met at the synagogue or visited with afterwards spoke German. They came from the same part of Europe the Szolds did, where the language and customs were German. The rabbi's sermon—a speech that included a lesson from the Bible—was always in German.

Henrietta, the Szolds' first child, was a healthy little

girl, but other children born in those days were not as lucky. Medicines like aspirin and penicillin had not yet been discovered, so many babies died.

When Henrietta was two years old, her sister Estella was born, but she was not strong, and she lived only a few months. Rebecca was born a year later, but she died, too. Henrietta missed having a baby to cuddle so much that when she found some chicks in her backyard, she treated them as if they were her babies. But she hugged them too hard and they did not live, either.

The Civil War was fought during those years, when Americans from the North and South fought over whether or not to permit slavery. Henrietta did not know any slaves, but her mother once showed her a place near their house where white people bought and sold black people.

When the family observed the holiday of Passover in the spring of 1865, they celebrated two freedoms. First, they remembered how, in the Bible, the Jews had been rescued from slavery in ancient Egypt. They also celebrated the end of America's Civil War, which gave freedom to all, both black and white. But during Passover week, they also heard that President Lincoln had been murdered.

Henrietta never forgot the day Lincoln's body

passed through Baltimore on the way to its grave in Illinois. Soldiers and important leaders were walking next to the horse-drawn carriage that carried his coffin through the city. Henrietta and her family and friends, watching from the large parlor window, saw them coming down the street. Walking among the important men of the city was Henrietta's own father. She was so proud!

As the years passed, Henrietta's wish for sisters finally came true. She was 5 when Rachel was born, 8 when Sadie arrived, and 11 when Johanna came. But there was another tragedy four years later when Johanna died of scarlet fever.

Henrietta had a hard time accepting these deaths. For a long time, she suffered from chorea, a twitching disease. On Henrietta's thirteenth birthday, Bertha was born. This baby helped fill the emptiness in Henrietta's heart. The last of the Szold sisters, Adele, was born the year Henrietta turned 16.

The girls had a lot of fun together. Together they would take their little white dog, named Sancho Panza, for long walks. They picked unusual flowers and then tested each other to see who could name them. They collected buttons and put them on a long string that they hung near the front door. No two buttons were the same, and, in a game they played, one button was called the "touch button." Visitors who happened to touch that one had to bring a new button for the chain on their next visit.

They spent a lot of time with their nearby neighbors, the Friedenwalds, and enjoyed long visits with their friends the Jastrows when they traveled to Philadelphia. They played piano and sang and danced. They loved mimicking people they knew and laughing together at their imitations. Their mother joined in and was especially good at it.

But Mrs. Szold was also a very serious and very organized person. She carefully taught her daughters how to run a home. They learned to cook, sew, manage household money, and care for each other.

Henrietta was often in charge, since she was the oldest. She was not always patient, and in a temper would yell at her little sisters. "I don't mind your using my ribbons or handkerchiefs," she would tell them, "but why must you make a mess of my bureau drawer?"

Henrietta loved taking care of her little sisters and she did her home jobs well. With her sharp mind, she learned German, Hebrew, and French, as her parents used these languages at home. But what she liked best was learning about her father's work. She was only 6 when he told her about a new prayer book he was writing, to explain the Hebrew prayers in new ways.

She loved the way he studied the Torah (the Jewish Bible) and the ideas about religion that he discussed in his sermons. They enjoyed their time together, and they felt closer to each other than to anyone else.

Life in those days was very different from the way it would be just a few years later. No one yet had electricity or telephones, cars or free public schools. Rabbi Szold wanted his children to learn more about the new modern world than he could teach them himself. He asked the congregation to hire a teacher for a class of children that would meet at the synagogue.

Good teachers were hard to find, and the one they hired was a bit strange and very strict. Jonas Goldschmitt met with his students in two rooms in the basement of the synagogue. Wearing slippers and a robe, he smoked a pipe while he taught English and German. He also carried a stick and hit the hand of any child who did not work hard. But it was not his stick that hurt Henrietta.

One day, Henrietta did not give him the answer he expected. He turned to her and said in German, "Und du, du, du, Szold?" "And you, you, you, Szold? Aren't you ashamed of yourself?" He had yelled at her this way because she was the rabbi's daughter. He had embarrassed her in front of all her friends. For the rest of her life, she remembered the pain of that moment.

Soon afterwards she did something else that caused her to be noticed and embarrassed. She knew her parents were going to see a show performed by a famous German actor. She wanted to go with them, but they could not afford another ticket. She went to speak to the actor himself.

Wearing her best pink dress and white straw hat, and carrying a brown parasol, she told him, proudly and in perfect German, who her father was. He gave her free tickets to the show, which had some bad language and was really meant for adults. Afterwards, he visited the Szold home. Little Henrietta waved her finger at him and said, "Didn't your mother teach you that it's bad to curse?" The story was reported in the newspapers and people accused her of being vain and rude.

Henrietta, who had been unfairly embarrassed these two times, never allowed it to happen again. For the rest of her long life, she was shy and quiet in public, and was careful in everything she said and did in front of others.

When Henrietta was 13, her family moved to a larger house on Lombard Street. Their new street was paved with red bricks and had fountains on the corners, where both people and their horses could stop for a drink.

On moving day, Rabbi Szold went to his new back-

yard. There he planted a vineyard and a fig tree. Planting, he said, was a way to plan for the future. For many years afterwards, the family ate figs on Rosh Hashanah, the Jewish New Year. They also used leafy grapevines from the vineyard to decorate the roof of their sukkah, a hut built for the fall holiday of Sukkot.

After the move to the new house, Henrietta began to attend Western Female High School. She studied languages and literature, math and astronomy. She was 14 years old, and for the first time, she was in school with girls her own age. And, also for the first time, she was the only Jew in the group. One day, she wrote a story to explain what America meant to

Jews. It was about two girls discussing a visit from George Washington's ghost. In the story, the Jewish girl explains, "We had no home. . . . Like orphans, who are pushed out in the cold world and made to suffer, so were we . . . until Washington, with his mighty hand, reared this temple to freedom," meaning America.

Rabbi Szold gave Henrietta a gold pin when she graduated at the top of her class. In her speech at the graduation, she explained how important she thought public schools were to new Americans. She felt that they were a place where people who were new to the country could meet each other and become Americans together. "Public education truly is the cause . . . of all the prosperity and harmony of our nation," she said.

The daughter of immigrants had become an American because of her education. She wanted everyone to have that chance.

# 2

# The Teenage Teacher

Henrietta's parents told her they couldn't give her a college education because they couldn't afford it. But she knew it was also because she was a girl.

In the 1870s, many people agreed that a college education might be important for a boy. But a girl would probably marry and spend her life at home caring for the family. There were a few girls who did go to college, but their education was considered a waste of time. After all, who needs a diploma to change diapers or cook soup? The rare woman who did not marry was called a spinster, and she was expected to help raise her relatives' children.

Henrietta had been a very good student at her high school. At the age of 16, just after graduating, she got a job as a teacher there. Some of her students were as old as she was. Many were taller, since she herself was rather short. No one had ever taught her how to teach. She learned by doing it. And because she was very smart and well organized, she was very good at it. The next year, she was invited to teach at the Misses Adams' School.

The Misses Adams—Ada, Loulie, and Charlotte Adams—were spinster sisters. They ran a school for daughters of southern families who were made poor by the Civil War. Henrietta taught languages, history, science, and math.

Henrietta usually woke up at 5 o'clock in the morning to organize her work. She spent most of the day teaching. Her evening hours she would spend on one of her favorite hobbies—writing letters to relatives and friends. Before going to bed, she would take a record book from a shelf over her desk and carefully write down all the money she earned and spent.

Writing down her opinions became so much fun that she began to write essays for *The Jewish Messenger*, a newsletter printed in New York. She also wrote the "Baltimore Letter," a column published in a San Fran-

cisco newspaper. But these she did not sign with her own name. She was afraid of being singled out and embarrassed again. She signed them "Shulamith," a name from the Bible.

Henrietta held strong opinions about religion, government, and the role of women, and wrote about them, often making her readers angry. One told her she was only "a pan and pot scourer," who should not have an opinion because she was a woman! She answered in a nasty tone that women should not forget to take care of their "more awkward fellow creatures," by which she meant men.

When Henrietta was 18, her mother took the youngest children to Europe to visit their family there. The oldest children stayed home with Rabbi Szold. When she was 21, Henrietta took the same trip with her father. She was glad she had learned German at home, so she could enjoy the people and culture of that part of Europe.

Her travels and all the hours she had studied with her father filled her with information. She loved discussing important ideas with the college men who came to visit the Szold home. These students enjoyed their conversations with Henrietta and her father almost as much as they loved the good kosher meals that came from Mrs. Szold's kitchen. And of course, they came to meet the rabbi's daughters.

Among the many young men visitors, two students from Philadelphia visited the Szolds often. One was Cyrus Adler, a scholar in both American and Jewish subjects. The other, Joseph Jastrow, was the son of their old family friends. He was interested in a new science, called psychology, that studied how people behave.

Henrietta loved to talk and argue with them about serious ideas like religion and current events. But she was a working woman already in her twenties. She did not have time to relax and laugh with them. When these men looked for women to marry, they did not consider her. Adler fell in love with Henrietta's Baltimore friend, Racie Friedenwald, and Jastrow married Henrietta's sister, Rachel.

During the 15 years that Henrietta taught and wrote, she also took classes at nearby Johns Hopkins University. There she discussed the idea of free school for everyone.

She suggested that a teacher should have no more than 25 children in a class, an idea she learned from the Talmud (Jewish law based on the Torah). She insisted that "life in the 20th century will not be easy to live, that it will call for high courage to face the truth."

She suspected that the next century would be especially difficult for Jews. The Russian government had already announced laws that decided where Jews could or could not live.

Beginning in 1881, there had been pogroms ("po-GRUMS") in eastern Europe, when Russians rioted against Jews. They beat them, stole their property, ruined their cemeteries, and burned their homes and synagogues. Jewish neighborhoods were destroyed, and many Jews were killed, but the government did not allow anyone to help them.

Jews began to leave Europe by the hundreds of thousands. Most came to the United States. Many arrived on ships that docked at the port in Baltimore. They were refugees, alone and afraid, without money or family. Rabbi Szold and his daughter met them at the port and helped them find homes and jobs.

How can they learn to get along in their new country if they cannot even speak English, wondered Henrietta. So she organized evening classes where new immigrants could come after working all day. There they studied English and shared advice about how to get along in America.

It was a new idea—no one had ever thought of having school for adults at night. In November of 1889, 30 students came to Henrietta's first night-school class. Twice that number came the second night and soon the school had hundreds of students.

Henrietta convinced other people to help. Racie's

father, Dr. Aaron Friedenwald, became chairman of the school committee. Louis Levin, a publisher, printed whatever worksheets the school needed. The Baltimore city government soon took over the program and it became the first official night school in the United States.

While the Szolds helped the refugees get settled, they heard their stories about anti-Semitism (Jew hating) in Europe. It was hard for them to believe the reports. Where the Szold family lived, Jews had lived in peace for many years. The Szolds were sure the Jews' problems in Europe would not last.

But suddenly anti-Semitism appeared in France. A

loyal army officer, Alfred Dreyfus, was accused of being a traitor, and was sent to prison. Years later he was proven innocent, but people had assumed he was guilty only because he was a Jew.

One reporter who wrote about the case was Theodor Herzl. He began to feel that Jews needed their own land—the land promised to them in the Bible. This would be the return to Jerusalem spoken of in Jewish prayers that were 2,000 years old. He told everyone about his idea of "Zionism," a movement to establish a Jewish homeland in Israel (then called Palestine). Many Jews agreed with this idea and became Zionists.

Henrietta loved the United States. It was her home and she felt safe and happy to be living in a free America. But knowing what her Russian Jewish students had been through made her think that the idea of a Jewish homeland was important. America would always be her country, but she believed all Jews should have a place to go when other countries did not want them.

Henrietta could not be concerned with Zionism just yet, though. She had to deal with a tragedy at home. In 1893, Henrietta's sister Sadie caught pneumonia and died at the age of 26, just before she was to be married. Her death was bad enough, but more bad news was on the way.

Rabbi Szold started getting terrible stomach pains. At the same time, his congregation told him they wanted a change. Oheb Shalom Synagogue was moving to a new building and its members wanted a younger rabbi who would be less strict with them. Rabbi Szold was forced to retire.

Bertha and Adele—who were permitted to go to college because opinions had begun to change—were away at school. Rachel was married and living in Wisconsin. It was up to Henrietta to help their mother care for their father. She gave up her jobs at both the Misses Adams' School and the night school.

But Henrietta was not going to be left without a job. Her friend Cyrus Adler had organized the Jewish Publication Society of America (known as JPS) in Philadelphia, to publish books on Jewish subjects. He asked Henrietta to be its editorial secretary. She could do this job either at the Philadelphia office or at home in Baltimore.

Part of her job was to edit and correct what other people wrote. But she did much more than that. She also translated entire books into English. She was in charge of editing the many volumes of the Jewish Encyclopedia, and wrote 15 of its articles.

As her father's health got worse, Henrietta did more of her work at home. In 1902, shortly after Bertha married Louis Levin, Rabbi Szold died.

Henrietta, who had loved him so dearly, missed him terribly. Her father had always been at the center of her life. What would she do without him? And what about all his work? It would be such a pity to lose his great wisdom.

She walked into his library and stared at his books. Then she realized what she must do. She would edit what he had written so it could be published. But she was afraid that she did not know enough to do a good job on such an important project.

She wrote to her friend Cyrus Adler, who was on the board of the Jewish Theological Seminary in New York. She wanted to study in its school for rabbis, even though no woman had ever been allowed to study there before. She was told she could, but on one condition—that she did not ever expect to become a rabbi.

In 1903, Henrietta, her mother, and her sister Adele moved to New York City, to an apartment across the street from the Seminary. She was 43 years old.

There, while she continued her work for JPS, she studied hard and worked on her project.

There, too, she finally met—and lost—the one man she could ever love.

# 3

# In and Out of Love

Times were changing. In 1903, new apartment buildings had electricity, and cars shared the road with horse-drawn carriages. Some people were beginning to think about a new idea that would take many years to build—a huge bridge, named for George Washington, across the Hudson River between New York and New Jersey.

Henrietta was trying to change, too. She wanted to forget the pain of her father's death. She decided to study hard for her project of publishing his work.

Her classes at the Seminary were not as difficult as

she had thought they would be. But there was one group of classes she worried about going to—the ones taught by the great scholar, Louis Ginzberg.

It was not because she was afraid the work would be too hard. And it was not because she would be the only woman in the class. It was because of his blue eyes.

When he looked at her, she could not concentrate. He taught Talmud, and she was afraid that maybe she did not know enough. She decided not to go to that class.

But he came looking for her. He did not speak English perfectly yet, he explained. He needed someone to translate a speech from German into English. He had heard that her translations were the best. Would she please do it for him?

She could not say no. She did the work and quickly gave it back to him the minute she saw him in the school hallway. It was months before she saw him again.

But one day, he came to her home to attend an English class she taught for some of the Seminary professors. Then he began to come to the Szold apartment just to visit, or to have dinner.

"I am 43 years old. He should not affect me this way," Henrietta told herself. She tried to behave as if he were just like anyone else.

During the summer, Louis went to Europe to visit

his family. Henrietta stayed in New York to do work for JPS, as well as to work on her project. At Sabbath dinners, she and her mother, sister Adele, and friends at the Seminary discussed Zionism.

Theodor Herzl died that summer at the age of 44. Many worried that Zionism had died with him. What would happen to the Jews of Europe now?

When school began again in the fall, Henrietta took many classes, but not Professor Ginzberg's. He might not like the idea of a woman in the room when he taught about marriage to men who would soon be rabbis. But when he saw her at a friend's home, he told her she would be welcome in his class. In fact, he asked her to please take notes on his English, so she could help him correct his mistakes.

Henrietta no longer wondered. She was sure that for the first time in her life she had fallen in love. She wrote lovingly about Louis in her diary. He was so much like her father, the only other man she had ever loved.

For the first time, she looked at herself the way she thought a man would, and she worried. What she saw was short, fat, and plain. Worst of all, she saw a woman 13 years older than the man she loved! She tried hard not to care about him, but she could not help it.

He often asked her to translate his letters or a chapter of a book he was writing into English. This was work she did for many of the professors, but for Louis she worked the way she had worked for her father—with love.

In the spring, they went for long walks along the Hudson River. He came to the Szold apartment for dinner and got along well with Henrietta's mother. He never spoke of love, never held her hand, never talked about the future.

Louis spent the summer of 1905 in Europe. He wrote to her about his ship rocking across the Atlantic. She wrote to him about a play she had read. He bought her gifts—a book and an inkwell.

She took his class in September. After class, they took long walks in Morningside Park. When it was windy, he tied her veil for her so her hat would not blow away. When she was sick, he bought her a pill box for her medicine.

In March, Louis learned his father had cancer. He told Henrietta he would have to go to Amsterdam to be with him. He was sad he could not please his father by marrying before the old man died. This worried Henrietta. Would he marry some young woman in Europe just to please his father?

But still they wrote letters. He told her how much her letters helped him through this terrible time of caring for his dying father. She told him about a discussion group she had joined, called the Hadassah

Study Circle. She explained that this group of young Jewish women met every week in a different member's home. They discussed Herzl's Zionism and studied Hebrew.

When Louis came back in the fall of 1907, they saw each other every day. After seeing them together like this for nearly four years, their friends began talking about them as if they were a couple, and wondered when they would marry.

Henrietta began to pray that, if he was ever going to marry her, it would be soon. She wanted to be young enough to have children.

In June, he left for Europe again, and again he wrote her letters. When he returned at the end of the summer, he came to see her right away. He had wonderful news! He was engaged to be married the following year to a woman from Berlin, a woman 14 years younger than himself.

What did he say? He was going to marry a woman young enough to be Henrietta's daughter? Henrietta could not catch her breath. She leaned against the wall and told him she hoped he would be very happy. After he left, she went to bed and stayed there for two days.

As if nothing were wrong, he came to visit the next week. He brought her a gift he had bought for her in Europe and invited her out for a walk.

Could it be he did not know how she felt about

him? He seemed completely innocent, she told her friends. Or maybe he *planned* to look innocent, she thought again.

She was so tired of being lonely, of taking care of her mother and sisters, of working so hard while others had happiness. She had given years of her life to others and was respected for what she accomplished—teaching, starting the night school, editing for JPS, studying at the Seminary. But it never seemed to be her turn to build a family of her own.

"Happiness for all but me," she wrote in her diary.

During her five years in New York, several men had asked her to marry them. She had said no because she did not love them. Now she knew she could never love anyone else. What would become of her?

In her diary, she wrote, "Why did I ever forget my age? Oh, I am not all wrong—he made me forget it."

She had to get away, as far away as possible. She asked for and was given a six-month vacation from her job at JPS. They also gave her a gift of $500, in thanks for all the fine work she had done for them.

She took her diary, all of Louis's letters, the veil he had helped her tie, and the pill box and book he had given her. She put them in a drawer and closed it.

Henrietta and her mother started packing for a trip that would take them as far away as possible—a trip that would take them to the other side of the world.

32

# 4

# Putting Hadassah to Work

Sixty years later, an airplane would be able to cross the Atlantic Ocean in only six hours. But in July of 1909, the passenger ship carrying Henrietta and her mother sailed for two weeks to get to Paris, France. For all that time, Henrietta thought about her lost love.

In her diary, she wrote: "I still feel bottled and corked. I cannot speak out to anyone as I did to him— nor could he to anyone as to me. That I will believe to my dying day."

The two women went on by train. They visited

relatives in Austria and Hungary. Henrietta was happy to tell them all about the freedoms of life in America—that she, a woman and a Jew, was respected for her work.

America sounds wonderful, they said. More and more, their lives in Europe were filled with the problems of anti-Semitism. People would not give jobs to Jews, or do business with them, or let the children attend certain schools.

Henrietta's heart ached for them, but she still had her mind on her own lost love. When she heard at last that Louis Ginzberg had gotten married, she felt crushed.

Enough! She must get on with her life, she thought, but how could she forget him if everyone and everything around her kept reminding her of him? She had to get away! Far, far away!

Henrietta and Sophie Szold packed their bags. Leaving family and comfort behind them, they began the journey of all journeys. They would make the trip most people in those years only dreamed about—a visit to the Holy Land.

As their train crossed Europe into Asia, the two American women felt the Middle East swallow them up. The train stations overflowed with noisy, dirty people speaking many languages. Filthy city streets were crowded with overloaded donkeys and sweating men, and beggars. On they traveled, south to the Holy Land.

This was the land that would become the State of Israel in 1948, but then it was a backward corner of the Turkish Empire called Palestine.

Some of Palestine's Jewish families had lived there since the days of the Bible. Many of them wanted to live only in places mentioned in the Bible, study holy texts, and grow old and die in the Holy Land. They lived on charity sent to them by Jews in Europe and America.

In the last 100 years, many more came because they were hated in Europe. Others came because of the poverty of life in Arab countries.

The newer Palestinian Jews had come in the 1880s, many of them running away from the pogroms of Russia and Poland. They arrived in Palestine at the same time that Henrietta and her father were meeting ships of refugees in Baltimore. These were the Zionist pioneers, the *halutzim* ("ha-loo-TSIM"), and they refused to live on charity.

The *halutzim* did not go to the ancient cities. Instead they bought land in the swamps, in the valleys, or on the rock-filled mountainsides. They planted fruit trees and grapevines, and started villages. They named the first town Petah Tikvah, meaning "gateway of hope." Others—like Tel Aviv—would someday be great cities.

These pioneers and their new farms and villages were known as the *Yishuv* ("Yee-SHUV"). This was what Henrietta wanted to see.

Henrietta looked from the window of the train as they neared Tiberias. She saw camel caravans and the black tents of the Arab nomads.

"We saw them fanning the grain as it was fanned in biblical times," she wrote in her diary. "We saw the maidens (. . . They were tattooed on their chins! . . .) go to the wells and carry jars of water home."

Henrietta first saw the Holy Land during the two-hour boat ride across Lake Kinneret, which is also called the Sea of Galilee. The town of Tiberias, with its black stone houses and filthy streets, shocked her. Thin, sick children were everywhere, with flies all around their infected, crusty eyes. The trachoma ("tra-KOH-ma") infection that made their eyes ooze had already made many of them blind.

Henrietta and Sophie were surprised to learn that a Jewish girls' school in the city of Jaffa had solved their trachoma problem. They taught their students how to keep their eyes clean. Those who were already

infected were treated with a new drug—sulfa—and blindness no longer cursed the students.

"If it was so easy, why not teach everyone how to protect the children's eyes?" Henrietta wondered. She explained to her mother how simple it would be to organize such a program for the whole country. This, her mother agreed, would be a wonderful project. Perhaps Henrietta's Hadassah discussion group in New York could organize it, she suggested.

At last it was time to go up to Jerusalem. Their train climbed up through the treeless, rocky hills. From the Mount of Olives, they looked out over the ancient walled city of Jerusalem on the next hill.

This was the place where the Bible says Abraham nearly sacrificed his son Isaac 4,000 years ago. On that site almost 3,000 years ago, the great Temple, home of the Jewish people, was built. On that ground 2,000 years ago walked a Jew named Jesus. The silver-domed El Aksa Mosque and gold-domed Mosque of Omar stand there still. They mark the spot where the Koran (the holy book of Islam) says that Muhammad, the founder of Islam, rose to heaven 1,300 years ago.

But Henrietta also saw how poor the people of Jerusalem were. For drinking water, rain was collected and sold in goatskins. No one filtered it to get rid of the germs. The smells of food, garbage, and dung filled the air. The buildings' stone walls were crowded with blind beggars. Many of them were children with trachoma.

"So much misery, so much to make the heart ache," wrote Henrietta in her diary.

Memories of how hard life was in the Holy Land haunted Henrietta on the voyage home. Why couldn't life be better there, she wondered. The Turks had a government, but they did not care about non-Turks. The British and French both wanted to rule Palestine. But the Turks, with Germany's help, would fight to keep it.

"The result," she wrote, "is that I am still a Zionist, that I think Zionism is a more difficult aim to realize than ever I did before." Then, thinking about the Jews in Europe, she wrote, "I am more than ever convinced that if not Zionism, then nothing, only death for the Jew."

On their trip home, Henrietta was startled to realize that she had not thought of Louis even once since arriving in the Holy Land. No, she decided, she had no time to spend on that. She had important work to do.

Henrietta spent the next eight months organizing American Zionists so they would be better able to help the *Yishuv*.

She brought together local women's study circles,

like her Hadassah study group, into an organization that would raise money for Palestine. This new group was named Hadassah in honor of the Hadassah of the Bible, who was also called Queen Esther. Her courage had saved the Jews of Persia from death.

Across the United States, Henrietta spoke to any group that would listen. She told them the good news first, about how the pioneers worked hard to grow crops on land that was dry and full of rocks, or buried under swamps.

Then she explained the rest of the truth.

"There is uncleanliness; there is narrow-minded charity. . . . There is disorganization."

When the Hadassah groups had their first convention in 1912, Henrietta was elected president. The group took as their motto a phrase from the prophet Jeremiah. In the Bible, he wrote: "Behold the voice of the cry of my people from a land that is very far off. . . . Is there no physician there? Why then is not the healing of the daughter of my people accomplished?"

To make their motto come true—"The healing of the daughter of my people"—they began raising money for projects. Their plans for Palestine included a visiting nurse service, a hospital, a nursery and pure milk service for newborn babies, and a school to train nurses. They decided that their projects would serve all the people of Palestine—Arabs, Christians, and Jews.

Within a few months, 10,000 of Palestine's children had been treated for trachoma. Henrietta and her Hadassah organization collected more money and began to plan a nursing school for the city of Jerusalem.

In 1914, a new kind of war began. For the first time, countries all over the globe were fighting a World War. Turkey and Germany, fighting on the same side, cut off all communication to Palestine. The help Hadassah was ready to send had to wait.

Just then, too, Sophie Szold became seriously ill. Once again, it became Henrietta's job to take care of someone she loved who was very sick. Sophie Szold died on August 6, 1917. Henrietta once again made the sad journey back to the cemetery in Baltimore, where she buried her mother next to her father and sisters.

In the same year that Sophie Szold died, the World War ended. When it was over, Great Britain ruled Palestine. That year, the British government issued the Balfour Declaration, which said it would be a good idea for the Jews to have a homeland in Palestine.

Better rulers than the Turks, the British improved roads and water supplies in Palestine. But they left many other things undone. Members of the *Yishuv,*

41

with the help of Hadassah and other groups, took over the job of starting schools and hospitals.

Hadassah members organized a group of American doctors, nurses, and medical supplies that would go to Palestine. Henrietta agreed to spend two years in Palestine, even though a doctor warned her that her heart was weak.

She packed what she knew she would need: cotton fabric for filtering water and mosquito netting to protect her at night. She took pants (which women her age did not wear in America) and waterproof shoes for wading across the Jordan River. She also packed her mother's Sabbath candlesticks and the gold pin her father had given her for graduation.

When Henrietta returned to Palestine in 1920, she found the war had left its people very poor and filled with hatred. The Arabs of Palestine believed that if they could push the Jews out, the British would give them the whole country to keep as their own.

The British had made too many promises to too many people. They decided to let the Arabs fight it out with the Jews. In 1920, Arabs rioted, shouting, "The government is with us!" They rioted again in 1929, 1935, and 1936. In Jerusalem, and in other cities, they wiped out whole Jewish neighborhoods.

Even after the riots, Henrietta believed there was hope for Jews and Arabs to live together in peace.

42

She disagreed with many leaders of the *Yishuv* on whether or not Palestine could be shared. They called her "the old lady," and sometimes wished she would keep her opinions to herself. Even so, they invited her to serve on the *Yishuv*'s committee of leaders.

She sometimes lost her temper with them. When they refused to cooperate or get organized, she would bang her fist on a tabletop and scream at them. When they disagreed over medical equipment or expenses, she would stamp her feet on the floor. During one meeting, she threw an inkwell across the room, walked out, and went home.

Henrietta rented an apartment overlooking the Mount of Olives. In all the years she lived in Jerusalem, she never bought a home or furniture. She kept her belongings in a trunk, because she believed she would soon return home—to the United States. She thought of herself as an American and met with other Americans often. She was always sure to celebrate the Fourth of July and Thanksgiving.

As she did all her life, Henrietta started every day at 5 A.M. with two hours of calisthenics, hair brushing, and bathing. Before her 20-minute walk to the office, she studied Hebrew. It bothered her that she could not speak that language as well as she spoke English.

The two years Henrietta had planned to stay in Palestine became three, then more. In 1928, Henrietta was 68 years old. By then, Palestine had electricity, a college, and 150,000 Jews in a hundred villages. But its one million Arabs convinced the British to stop allowing Jews into the country.

This was the saddest decision of all. Just when most countries—including the United States—began to refuse immigrants, Europe's Jews were running for their lives.

# 5

# A Mother of
# Thousands

The world's nightmare was beginning. By 1932, the
Nazis had become the most popular political party in
Germany. A year later, Adolf Hitler became head of
the government.

Hitler claimed that white, blond, blue-eyed Ger-
mans were the "master race." He said his "master
race" would rule the world. He established concentration camps where the "master race" could send the
handicapped and the retarded and anyone else who
was different—especially Jews.

The Jews of Europe had lived with anti-Semitism for many years, but they did not believe that Hitler would ever be allowed to carry out his plans. No one believed this new anti-Semitism would last very long.

In the 1930s, many Jews tried to get away from a Europe that did not want them. But they found out that other countries—including the United States—had limits on how many Jews they would allow into the country.

The one group that wanted them was Palestine's *Yishuv.* But the British government was afraid of the one million Arabs there, so they permitted only a few hundred Jews in at a time. As time went on, they let in fewer and fewer.

Many of Europe's Jews had lost their jobs—because they were Jews—and had trouble buying food for their families. Hungry teenagers wanted to work, but no one would hire them. Their parents worried about what their future might be.

In 1932, one Jewish mother in Germany had an idea. Recha Freier wrote to Miss Szold in Jerusalem: If a group of teenagers could be trained to do farm work, could the Jews of Palestine give them a place to live until this wave of anti-Semitism passed?

No, said Miss Szold, who already had more problems than she could handle. She was trying to get teachers for 10,000 children in the *Yishuv* who had never been to school. She was busy with teenage criminals and starving babies. Like most of the world, she could not know what terrible danger the Jews of Europe would soon face.

As usual, other leaders of the *Yishuv* disagreed with her. They said that Hitler's policies made this project urgent. One who felt strongly about it was her good friend Chaim Arlosoroff, a poet and politician. When he died suddenly, Henrietta decided to honor his memory by accepting the German children. When she wrote to her sisters about the new project, she said, "I should have had children—many children." So perhaps these would be like her own.

Henrietta knew well the poor conditions of the pioneers of the *Yishuv*. She saw the victims of Arab riots and killings. But now she began to understand that, as hard as life was in Palestine, Jews were safer there than in Europe.

The first group of children arrived in Haifa by ship in February of 1934. Henrietta and her assistants were there to meet them. She spoke to each one and took them to a settlement where they could live and work. She offered them the love of a grandmother, and they were glad to have it.

For the next eight years, she met every group that came in from all over Europe. The children kept coming, even when World War II began in 1939.

In that same year, the Nazis declared war on the world. The "master race" also began its war against the Jews. Men, women, and children were rounded up like cattle. Some were shot on the spot. Whole towns were emptied of Jews, who were stuffed into railroad boxcars and sent to concentration camps to become slaves or to be used for experiments. The weak ones died early; the strong ones lasted a few years.

The United States did not enter the war until 1941. By then, the Nazis had begun a system of death camps. In those camps, thousands of Jews and others—including people who were blind, retarded, or crippled, or those who were homosexuals, or those who were not white—were killed every day. Their bodies were burned and their bones thrown into pits. This Nazi system of killing was later named "the Holocaust," which means "completely destroyed by fire."

By the end of the war and its Holocaust in 1945, the Nazis would murder 11 million people. Six million of those were Jewish, and one-and-a-half million of the Jews were children. But Henrietta never knew how bad it was. The world learned most of the facts after the war, months after Henrietta's death.

As the war got worse, some children escaped and came by themselves. These young children had no group, no training, and no plan. Henrietta met them, had them checked by doctors, and found them a home.

The largest group of children that Henrietta brought into Palestine included 933 who came through Teheran, Persia, in 1942. Many of these children had been only four or five years old in 1939, when they were separated from their families. Many had seen their parents dragged off to death camps or shot in their homes. Older children carried younger ones as they wandered across Europe. For more than three years, they hid like animals in forests or in barns, eating and sleeping when they could.

By the time they reached Teheran, they were like frightened, filthy, wounded animals. People from the *Yishuv* came to help them. They gave them food and told them they would soon be "home" in the Holy Land.

Henrietta did not realize until she saw them arrive in Haifa what deep sorrow this group of children brought with them.

They wore cut-down adult clothes and broken soldiers' helmets. Some were so sick they had to be carried. Most could not remember their parents' faces. They were so scared of what the next minute might bring that they refused to take off their clothes at night. They clutched leftover food tight in their hands, afraid someone would take it away.

Henrietta spent her last years trying to comfort these orphans. She hoped that, in their new homes, they would remember how to laugh and learn how to play. She visited her children as often as she could, bringing them flowers or a doll.

The project of saving the children was known as Youth Aliyah. "Aliyah" ("a-lee-YAH") is the Hebrew word for "going up." It is used to describe someone who goes to the Land of Israel. Youth Aliyah saved 15,000 children who came from Europe during the war. It also took care of those who were born in the *Yishuv* during those years, and who needed help. When Henrietta visited her children, they would talk and play and sing and dance—all the things parents or grandparents do with the children they love.

But in 1943, when she was 83 years old, she became too sick to travel around the country. To treat her pneumonia, doctors gave her the first shot ever given in Palestine of the newly discovered medicine, penicillin. She felt better, but was still very sick. They moved her into Hadassah Hospital, where she stayed at the nurses' school that she had helped organize on Mount Scopus, in Jerusalem.

Henrietta hated not being able to take care of herself. One of the Teheran children came to brush her hair every day. Henrietta complained, "Did I bring this girl here so that she might wait on me?"

Then she admitted, "I have always thought that with growing old I would become more rational, less bound to lose my temper."

Even from her bed, Henrietta was busy. She set up a fund for a research center on youth. Years later, the fund was named for her. On a two-way radio, she was awarded a Doctor of Humanities degree from Boston University. The New York Times called her the "grand old lady of Palestine." The Baltimore Sun called her "the foremost Jewish woman of modern times." In Palestine, she was known as the "mother of the *Yishuv.*"

Henrietta died on the evening of February 14, 1945. Thousands of her children came to the funeral. Some of them, who had arrived in Palestine as teenagers in the 1930s, brought their own children. In a way, these were Henrietta's grandchildren.

One of the Teheran boys led the "Kaddish," the prayer said by Jews when a close relative has died.

They buried her in the cemetery on the Mount of Olives, near where she and her mother had stood the first time they saw Jerusalem. She was buried in a grave there, which can no longer be found.

# 6

# The Mystery of Her Grave

Henrietta died just three months before the Second World War ended. She never knew how horrible the Nazi Holocaust had been, never knew that most of the Jewish children who were not rescued by Youth Aliyah had been murdered.

Europe's Jews who survived the war had no place to go. As people of the world learned how strong Hitler's anti-Semitism had become, they began to accept the idea of Jews having a country of their own, in Palestine.

In November of 1947, the United Nations voted

to divide Palestine. Part would become an Arab state and the rest would be the Jewish State of Israel. But the Arabs did not want part of Palestine, they wanted all of it.

In May of 1948, Israel declared its independence. The surrounding Arab countries attacked. When the war was over, the Jews had their state, but its border cut through Jerusalem. The newer areas were part of Israel, but the Old City was taken over by the Arab Kingdom of Jordan. Also in Jordan's control were Mount Scopus and the Hadassah Hospital and nursing school, where Henrietta Szold died, and the Mount of Olives, where she was buried.

The Israelis captured the Old City of Jerusalem and its nearby hills in the Six Day War in 1967. They found that the Arabs had built a road through the cemetery on the Mount of Olives. They had destroyed many of the grave markers. There was no longer any way to find Henrietta Szold's grave.

In 1968, a new stone to mark her life and death was placed next to the road in the cemetery, near where she had been buried. In the crowd of people who came to its dedication were Israel's leaders, Hadassah members from around the world, and hundreds of Youth Aliyah children.

To honor her efforts to improve health and education for the *Yishuv*'s pioneers, Israel put her picture on their money and on a postage stamp.

In Baltimore, Henrietta was honored for the invention of night school for immigrants. A street was named after her and her portrait was hung on a wall of the University of Maryland.

To honor her founding of the Hadassah women's Zionist organization, a street was named for her on New York's Lower East Side.

Today, the nearly 400,000 members of Hadassah around the world raise money for hospitals and schools. They serve the Jews, Moslems, and Christians of Israel.

Youth Aliyah was just one of Hadassah's projects begun by Henrietta Szold. The program has already helped nearly half a million children live healthy, happy lives. In this way, all of them are Henrietta's children.